ING

5 6/
lb.
bag

Chips

z. bags

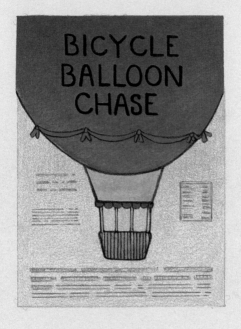

BICYCLE
BALLOON
CHASE

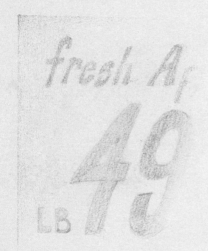

fresh Ai

49

LB

ri. 9:30 - 10:00
at. 9:30 - 6:00
Sun. closed

The Great Town and Country BICYCLE BALLOON CHASE

story by BARBARA DOUGLASS
pictures by CAROL NEWSOM

Lothrop, Lee & Shepard Books • New York

For the newest Douglass, ANNA LOUISE,

and for BOB,

whose help this time was
above and beyond the call of duty,

and for MOM and DAD,

who got me started on this
lifelong love affair with books.

LIBRARY OF CONGRESS
CATALOGING IN PUBLICATION DATA

Douglass, Barbara, (date). The great town and
country bicycle balloon chase. Summary: After
studying the short cuts in town, Gina and Grandpa
hope to win the bicycle balloon chase, but just as
they sense victory, they start chasing a parrot in-
stead of the balloon. [1. Bicycle racing—Fiction.
2. Balloons—Fiction] I. Newsom, Carol, ill.
II. Title.
PZ7.D7479Gr 1984   [E]   83-14877
ISBN 0-688-02231-6
ISBN 0-688-02232-4 (lib. bdg.)

"What does that mean?" Gina asked Grandpa,
pointing to the poster.

It was the third one she'd seen that week.

"What's a bicycle balloon chase?"

The mechanic in the bike shop
told them all about it.
"A big hot-air balloon will
be launched in the park
this Saturday.
Only the wind knows which
way it will go.

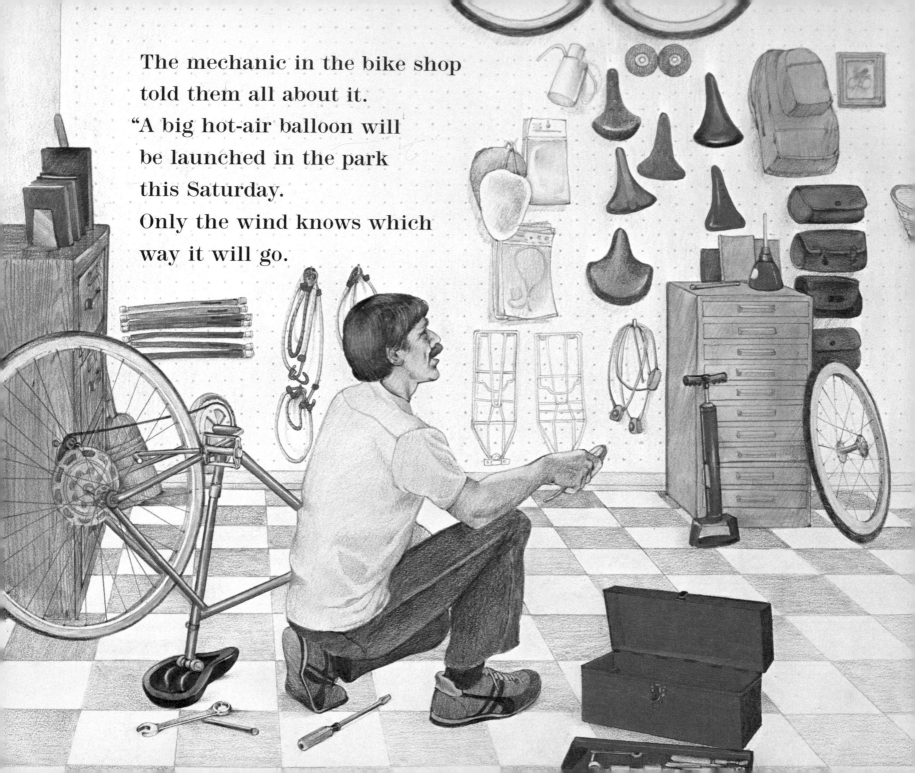

But we'll follow it on
our bikes and after it lands,
the first two bikers who
get close enough to touch it
will win a free ride
in the balloon."

For the rest of the week Gina and Grandpa
pedaled all over town.
They rode uphill on Main Street.
They rode downhill on Maple Street.

Gina counted five more posters.

Grandpa counted shortcuts.

"If only the wind knows which way the balloon will go," he said,

"we have to know the shortest way to everywhere."

On Saturday Gina and Grandpa were up before sunrise.
After breakfast Gina packed apples and peanuts
while Grandpa pumped air in their tires.
At last Grandpa put on his cap and said,
"I do believe we're ready.
Let's go chase that balloon."

On their way to the park Gina saw cars with bicycles on the front.

She saw cars with bicycles on the back.

She saw cars with bicycles on the top.

But she didn't see a balloon.

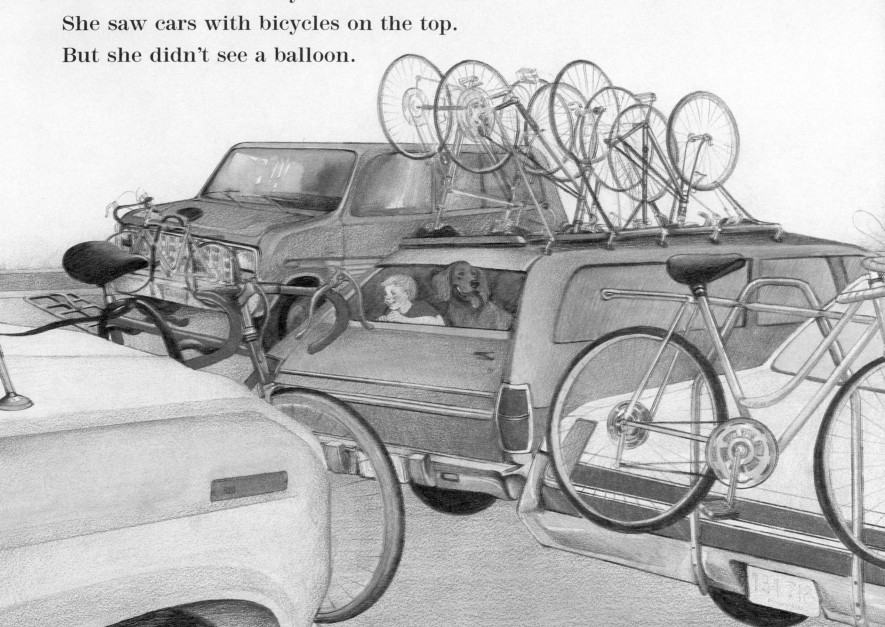

In the park she saw bicycles with great big front wheels
and little tiny back wheels.

She saw bicycles with two seats and four pedals.

She saw bicycles with only one wheel.

But she didn't see a balloon.

She saw babies in trailers, a poodle in a handlebar bag,
and a woman with a parrot in the back of a pickup truck.
"Where's the balloon?" asked Gina.
"Look in the back of that truck," Grandpa told her.
"The woman is an aeronaut, the basket is a gondola,
and the balloon is in the bag."
"But I thought it was a BIG balloon," said Gina.
"It will be," said Grandpa. "Watch and see."

Gina watched.

The aeronaut and her helpers unloaded the truck.

They set the gondola on the grass and tipped it over.

They opened the bag and pulled out a bundle of

green, red, purple, and blue,

and they unrolled it

    and unrolled it

        and unrolled it.

The long, skinny bundle had a big mouth.

Helpers held it open.

The aeronaut turned on a fan.

The bundle stretched and wriggled.

It wriggled and it grew.

The aeronaut turned on a burner.

The balloon
gobbled fire
and grew higher
and higher and higher.
Finally it stood up
straight and tall.
Taller than ten buildings stacked
one on top of another.

"Ready?" called the aeronaut.
"Ready!" answered the bikers.
The helpers let go of the ropes.
The balloon floated up and away.

No one knew which way to go.

A man on a penny-farthing bike said, "I think the wind will blow the balloon this way. Let's take Main Street."

A woman on a unicycle said, "I think the wind will blow the balloon that way. Let's take Maple Street."

A man and a woman on a tandem bike said, "This way," and, "That way," both at once.

They took a spill.

Grandpa took a shortcut.

Gina followed Grandpa.

When the balloon drifted this way, Grandpa took this shortcut.

When the balloon drifted that way, Grandpa took that shortcut.

Gina followed Grandpa through every shortcut in town.

The balloon drifted lower and led them into the country.

It led them past the Carlsons' dairy,

where it made the cows stumble and bellow.

It led them past the Souzas' farm,
where it made the sheep scramble and bleat.
It led them past the Hosangs' ranch,
where it made the horses gallop and whinny.
Then it drifted even lower.

It led them to a field of clover.

"Hurry, hurry," said Gina to Grandpa.

"I think we might be first!"

But the aeronaut called, "Whoops! Beehives!

We'll have to look for a better place."

The burner hissed fire, and the balloon rose again.

Grandpa and Gina pedaled faster.
When the balloon dipped down over another field
they were ready to run and touch it.

But the aeronaut called, "Whoops! A bull!
We'll have to look for a better place."
The burner hissed.
The bull roared.
The parrot squawked in fright.
The aeronaut called, "Oh, no! Gypsy! You come back here!"

The parrot flew this way.
The balloon blew that way.
Gina followed the parrot.
Grandpa followed Gina.
All the other bikers followed the balloon.

The parrot didn't take
any shortcuts.
It led them right
through the Hosangs' ranch,

All the way around
the Souzas' farm,

and clear across the Carlsons' dairy
before it landed on a giant sunflower
and Gina climbed up and caught it.

Quickly, Gina and Grandpa turned their bikes around.
They pedaled hard. They pedaled fast.
They pedaled harder and faster than ever
past the dairy
    and the farm
        and the ranch.

They were the last ones to reach the balloon.
The winners were ready to take their ride.
The burner hissed.
The balloon tugged at the ropes.
Gypsy flew back where he belonged.

Suddenly the aeronaut called to her helpers.
"Wait! Don't let go yet."

She pointed to Gina and Grandpa and said,
"Please put your bicycles in the back
of our chase truck and come over here."

They did, and the aeronaut explained,
"There's room in the gondola for two more bikers.
And anyone who is smart enough to catch my runaway parrot
should have a chance to go up in my balloon.

"Welcome aboard!"